OWL at SCHOOL

for Rebecca

OWL at SCHOOL

by Helen Nicoll
and Jan Pieńkowski

PUFFIN BOOKS

The
first
lesson
was
swooping
and
pouncing

WHOOSH

The bell rang for dinner

They all had different food

Mole
in the hole

Shrew
stew

Ms Bats taught night flying

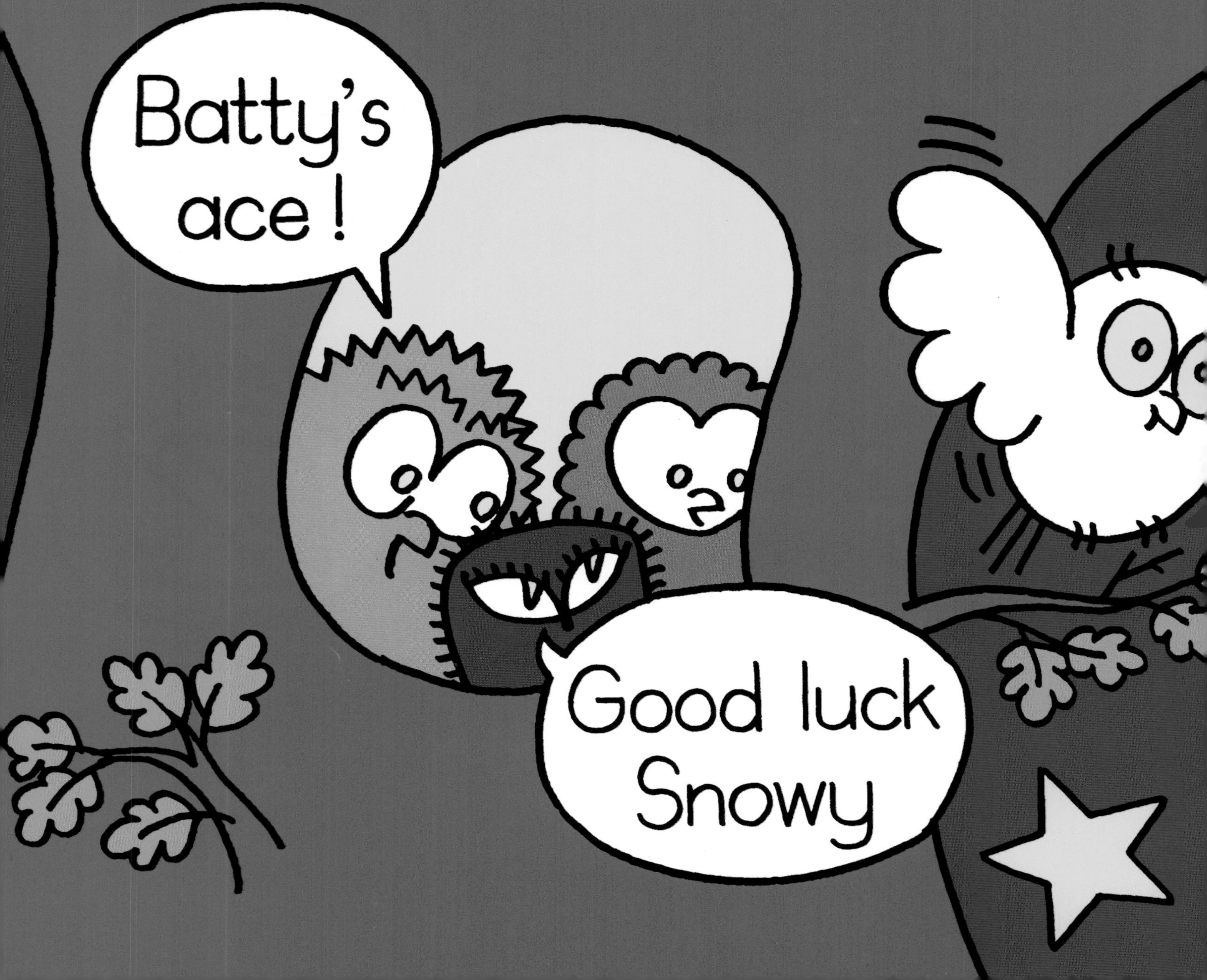

good
at
diving

and
bottom
in
swimming

Meg
brought
Mog
to watch
the
School Sports

Everybody noticed Meg's hat

Owl won the night flight race

After tea they all went home

Goodbye!